C000092869

ISLAND SUN

ESCAPE TO THE ISLANDS

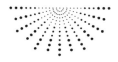

HOLLY GREENE

Copyright © Little Blue Books, 2019

The right of the author to be identified as the Author of the Work
has been asserted by her in accordance with the Copyright,
Designs and Patents Act 1988.

All rights reserved. No part of this publication may be reproduced,
stored in a retrieval system, or transmitted, in any form or by any
means without the prior written permission of the author. You
must not circulate this book in any format.

All characters in this publication are fictitious and any
resemblance to real persons, living or dead is purely coincidental.

"To Ellie Moore, my annoyingly lucky best friend," Maria said, holding up a bottle of beer, a grin on her face. "Congratulations for landing not just your dream job, but one with a guy who is probably the most talented, but *definitely* the hottest chef on TV."

Everyone on the roof terrace of the San Francisco townhouse held up their drink and hollered out to Ellie. She blushed and raised her own glass in return as the night sky pulsed from the Golden Gate Bridge across the water.

It was chillier than usual in the city for September, and she zipped up her jacket to fight the shivers that were a combination of both cold and nerves.

She was excited but also more than a little overwhelmed about her new job, and there were a lot of things she had to do to get ready for her first day on Monday. Her best friend's party was a welcome distraction.

Zack Rose...

She was *actually* going to work for Zack Rose— internationally acclaimed chef, cookbook author and TV personality. A bona-fide international celebrity with over *twenty million* social media followers.

The thought that Ellie would share the same planet as the guy, let alone be one of his employees, seemed laughable, but it was true.

It had taken three rounds of interviews, but she had done it, knocking out a plethora of other applicants and landing a much sought-after marketing position with his media company.

"So what's he like?" Maria asked, beer in hand as she sat beside Ellie on the outdoor sofa.

"Who - Zack?"

Her friend nodded enthusiastically, but her eyes were slightly vacant, indicating she had already imbibed a few Bud Lights for the evening, which on her small frame would carry her well through the night.

Ellie shrugged. "I only met him briefly during the interview process and we haven't really talked."

"Never mind that - is he as hot as he looks on TV?"

Ellie didn't want to burst Maria's bubble, but she didn't want to lie to her best friend either.

"Yes and no. You know how he looks so tanned onscreen and has perfect white teeth? In reality, he looks a lot older, his skin is absurdly orange and his teeth look like they've been bleached white about five times too many. That alone you'd probably be able to get past, but he's also *super* skinny. On TV he looks normal and healthy, but in person... he's almost scrawny."

Maria nodded slowly as if she had just heard something deep and spiritual, but in actuality was just trying to not appear as drunk as she was.

"Is he seeing someone?" she asked, evidently unfazed by anything Ellie had just told her.

She laughed. "I don't know. I just got the job a couple of weeks ago and I don't start until Monday. I know as much as you do about his personal life. Probably less, I expect."

Scott, a mutual friend, plopped down on the other side of her declaring, "Ellie's going to hook us up with all the celebs!" He gestured to everything on the roof. "And soon, instead of eating takeout Magiano's here, Zack Rose himself will be catering our little get-togethers."

He held out his fist for Maria to bump, but she didn't get it and left him hanging.

Ellie giggled and did it for her. "Um... don't get your hopes up guys," she said dubiously. "At most, maybe I'll be able to get you a signed cookbook for Christmas."

"You're in denial," Maria slurred. "You need to accept your own worth. You and I are not the same pimply-faced graduates in tens of thousands in debt anymore. You're shit-hot marketing guru Ellie Moore, and only... I don't know what your debt is anymore but I imagine it's much less now. You're moving on up sweetie, and now your world is about to look a whole lot different. Are you ready?"

"I think so," Ellie replied sheepishly, clinking glasses with her friends.

But was she?

CHAPTER TWO

*T*he following Monday, Ellie arrived at Zack Rose's media complex an hour early so she could have time to organise her desk and acclimate to her new surroundings.

The media offices/studio comprised a bland concrete building about fifteen minutes away from the city.

This had surprised her each time she went in for a follow-up interview. For an A-list celebrity/business tycoon, Zack Rose apparently had no problem working in a generic office building on a forgetful street.

Ellie never brought it up, but the guy himself did during the first interview:

"I'm a self-made man and as such, I understand the

value of money," he said in his English accent, but with that faint Mediterranean twinge that belied his Greek roots.

"I could afford something ten times better than this place, but I'm not willing to spend the money on it, and I wouldn't be the man I am today if I did. So I think very carefully about what I consider necessary, and what I consider frivolous. I surround myself with the best people I can find, and I'm willing to pay top dollar for them because I know at this point in my life that if I didn't I'd be wasting my money— and I *hate*, notice I'm using the word *hate* - I *hate* wasting money. I tell you this so you know how important this is to me. Are you, Ellie, the best in your field? Will hiring you be the best use of my money? Or will I be flushing it down the toilet if I do?"

Ellie hadn't specifically prepared for this question during her practice interviews, but she knew right off the bat how she would handle it.

Without hesitation, she looked him confidently in the eye and said, "I am the best you'll find, and I'm the best investment of your money because—"

She believed how she handled that question is what landed her the job— in particular her use of the word *investment*.

In the marketing world, confidence, real or otherwise, was how you persuaded people, Ellie knew.

Whether what she said was true or not, well…

When she pulled into the attached parking garage she noticed that there was already a handful of cars present. Things were already in full swing at— she checked her watch— 6:55 am.

Inside the building, a small, bespectacled rat-like man appeared out of the shadows when she came through the door, and put a finger to his lips. He made circling motions in the air to indicate that they were recording in an adjoining studio.

Ellie nodded and proceeded to tiptoe past, but the small man stopped her again. He mimed to her that she needed to take off her heels before he would allow her to walk any further.

She slipped them off, and the unnamed sentry walked her to the media offices in the back.

Treading lightly, she got a glimpse of Zack Rose in-studio on the way. Spiky blond hair, artificially tanned skin, glowing white teeth, he was kneading dough and talking continuously as he did:

"I know it's a pain to work with, but we're not making pizza dough here. It's got to be a little sticky. Add too much flour to make it easier on yourself, and you will have botched the whole process. Your dough

7

will be too thick for pasta. If that happens or has already happened, put it aside. You may as well make pizza with it later. Just hit pause, rewind, I'll still be here, smiling like this— " he walked up to the camera and gave an extra long, sarcastically wide smile and stopped still.

As he was pretending to be frozen, he caught a glimpse of Ellie looking at him when she walked by. It was only a moment, but she thought she saw a flicker of annoyance in his eyes. It quickly faded as he held up the dough one more time to the cameras.

The sentry opened a door for her and they both walked into the cubicled office.

The man eased the door closed behind them before turning around.

"I'm so sorry," Ellie blurted. "I didn't know he recorded this early. I thought I was going to be the first one in."

"Mr. Rose begins his days very early. Tomorrow, if you choose to arrive at the same time, I would ask that you walk around and enter from the street entrance. It's not convenient, but Mr. Rose hates to be distracted while he's recording." Then he bowed to her and added, "Good day, Miss Thomson, and good luck. I hope *you* last longer than the others."

He left, making sure he eased the door closed again with only a whisper.

Others? How many others have there been? Ellie wondered, gulping.

SHE FOUND her cubicle and unloaded her small bag of stuff on the desk. She booted up her laptop and as she was arranging her things, she heard someone else approach quietly.

They stepped slowly and softly as if they were afraid they might trip off an alarm.

A lean, muscular man peered at her and Ellie recognised him as the lead member of the existing marketing team Jeff Welch. He had been at all of her interviews.

"Oh *Ellie*," he whispered, smirking. "You didn't come in through the parking garage did you?" He seemed to think it was hilarious.

She nodded, gulping afresh.

Jeff scrunched up his face and shook his head dramatically. "Whatever you do, don't do *that* again. He'll probably let it fly today, but next time—"

"Walk around and come in through the front. Someone already told me."

Jeff relaxed a little. "It's not a big deal," he continued, flitting around her work area, picking up a picture of her and Maria and looking at it, before quickly losing interest and putting it back. "He just gets into his groove and doesn't like to be taken out of it." He smiled wide and asked, "So - excited for your first day?"

Ellie smiled back and said that she was.

"Good. Just a heads up; Z the great and powerful, has arranged something fun to start you off. Do you have a passport, by any chance?"

"I..." This took Ellie completely off guard. "Yes, but not with me. It's somewhere in my apartment. Why? Where am I going?"

"I'll let Big Z explain it to you. First, I've got to arrange some coffee. He should be done in a few minutes."

Ellie wanted to call Maria and sob that she'd messed up her first day already, especially when she saw more staff start trickling in through the front entrance. No one at all came in via the door she had been escorted through.

They all knew better.

Just then, the boss himself barged in briskly with a towel wrapped around his neck. "Ellie. Ellie Thomson," Zack shouted. "My office - now."

Her heart stopped. Crap, I'm getting fired already.

CHAPTER THREE

*E*llie walked across the hall to Zack's office, certain she was about to be yelled at, berated and finally, fired. He motioned for her to close the door and sit down.

"You speak Greek, yes?" he barked without preamble, walking with the towel still around his neck.

"Yes," she said, afraid to add that she'd studied it years ago in college but wasn't exactly fluent.

"Still fluent?" her new boss asked as if reading her mind.

Ellie thought about fudging but decided against it. "No, not really. Not enough practice."

He shrugged. "It doesn't matter. Everyone speaks

English over there anyway. Everyone relevant, anyway."

Over where?

"I'm sorry, I don't understand," she asked. "I thought I was on the marketing team to help expand your business?"

"Yes, that's right. *Which* is why you're going to Crete," he said theatrically, wiping his face with his towel. "As you know, I was raised in England," he continued, his voice muffled through the material, "and by all accounts I'm English— as you can no doubt tell from my accent. But my parents are Greek, and our family lived in Crete before my father got a job in London. As you also know, my book sales are astronomical around the globe, my show's TV ratings are sky-high, and last month I opened a restaurant in Mexico City against everyone's best advice— all thinking it was the most idiotic thing I'd ever done— and yet it's booked every night for the rest of the year! The third restaurant I opened up here on the West Coast is the same— solid bookings. By all accounts, I should be a happy man and *you*," he emphasised, "should have an easy job. But there's one place I'm not famous, Ellie. One place where my food is ignored, my books overlooked and my TV ratings non-existent. I'll give you a dime if you can guess where."

"Greece? Crete, even?"

Zack flicked an imaginary coin over to Ellie and she pretended to catch it, at which he smiled for a moment and she relaxed a little.

"The place of my forefathers couldn't care less about me. I want a piece of that market - a big piece. If anyone notices and decides to bring to attention that my own people think my food is crap, then my empire crumbles overnight." He snapped his fingers to emphasise. "And I need you to get over there and stop that from happening."

"There's no way they don't like your food," Ellie argued and shook her head. "I've always watched your show and ate at your restaurants every chance I could get. Your modern take on Mediterranean food is amazing. Nobody could ever say it's … crap."

Zack smiled wide— he apparently liked compliments, which Ellie realised was probably why the lack of attention in Greece wasn't so much a business gap, but a major blow to his ego.

"So you're going to Crete," he continued. There's a restaurant in Hersonissos called Thasos. Every night it's packed just like my own, and people fly in from all over the world just to go to there. I need you to figure out why it's so popular because together…" he paused for dramatic effect, "we're going to take it down."

HOLLY GREENE

Ellie's eyes widened.

"People need to be flying to Crete to go to *my* place, not theirs. I'm going to open up a rival restaurant that will make everyone forget all about this Thasos, and you're going to lay the groundwork for that. Understood?"

Ellie nodded, understanding that her first task for Zack's company would be a form of corporate espionage.

She could do it though; a major part of her skills was zoning in on something successful, understanding exactly what made it so and then replicating the results.

Marketing 101.

"It's a big job," Zack continued. "And a bloody important one to me, but I trust you with it. I know you can do it. I had a feeling about you the first time I met you."

"I won't prove you wrong," Ellie said determinedly.

Zack nodded as if he already knew this. "Jeff will arrange your tickets and will be going along with you. I've already pulled a few strings and got you both a reservation at Thasos on Thursday night after you fly in."

"Thursday this ... week?" she clarified, taken aback.

Her boss looked up sharply. "Will that be a problem? Any family members you need to deal with or a boyfriend, perhaps?"

"No, there's no one like that. Won't be a problem."

Zack nodded and motioned that they were done. She was at the doorway of her office when she heard him add, "Welcome to the team."

Ellie beamed. A trip overseas to an idyllic island in the sun on her very first week?

Maybe working for Zack Rose wouldn't be so bad after all.

CHAPTER FOUR

*S*he spent the rest of the day researching the Cretan restaurant scene and reviewing Thasos' menu.

The restaurant's offerings seemed pretty standard Mediterranean fare and the ingredients used were certainly nowhere near as innovative or imaginative as Zack's.

Yet reviews across the board were stellar, suggesting there was something more to this place than met the eye.

Many reviewers claimed it was the best dining experience of their lives, and a few even claimed to have had healing experiences there (whatever that meant).

And aesthetically Thasos was beautiful—no

surprise if Zack considered it a serious rival. Judging from the pictures on its website, and its geographical position on Google Earth, the restaurant could not have been located at a better spot on the island.

Not only did the crystal clear Aegean waters glimmer on the horizon in a lot of the shots taken from customer tables, but it was also right in the heart of Hersonissos, a popular Cretan tourist town.

Whoever owned the place must be swimming in money, Ellie thought.

The exterior of the building was interesting in an avant-garde sort of way. It seemed to be paying homage to Greece's past with sandstone blocks and arm-wide columns and was either designed to incorporate an iconic Greek structure of the distant past or made to look as if it did.

Architecture aside though, whoever had decorated the interior had avoided the common pitfall most other clichéd Greek tavernas fell into: there was not a single statue anywhere in the restaurant.

Smart, Ellie thought.

Subconsciously the restaurant seemed to tell each of its customers that it was offering something different, something unexpected from other traditional Greek tourist eateries. That people shouldn't go to Thasos if they were looking for a shish kebab and a

Corona. This place was authentic through and through, and despite herself, Ellie was already excited about eating there.

If Zack truly wanted to compete with Thasos on level terms, from what little she had already gathered, he would have his work cut out for him.

She leaned back in her chair. In truth, she didn't even need to visit in person to know that Thasos would be a seriously difficult rival to topple. She had enough experience in the business world to tell apart the barkers from the biters.

To compete with a restaurant of this calibre, one as popular and established with tourists and locals alike was going to require more than just skill.

Ellie sighed, understanding that her upcoming jaunt to Crete would certainly be no vacation.

CHAPTER FIVE

*I*t would be an overstatement to say that Ellie hated flying, but it did make her extremely uncomfortable because of her height— at six feet, there was just nowhere to put her feet.

The farthest she had ever flown was from San Francisco to New York City. It was roughly a six-hour flight, and she'd felt bruised and beaten afterwards.

Compare that to the coming trip to Athens, which including connections was estimated at sixteen and a half hours... and then onwards to Crete.

Sixteen and a half ever-loving hours. Maybe she could use the time to brush up on her Greek and re-read *The Stand*. Hell, she'd probably have time to finish the famously long Stephen King tome *and* be fluent in Greek by the time they landed.

So when the evening before they left, Jeff showed up at her desk with a pair of business class tickets, and she nearly wept with delight.

"Seriously?" she asked her new work colleague, not able to hide her awe and surprise.

"Honey, we're too tall to fly coach," he said theatrically, then leaned in and whispered, "Zack would probably throw a hissy fit if he knew, but... I'm not going to tell if you don't." Then he winked and flounced back to his own office.

Ellie could have kissed him but doubted the guy would get anything out of it.

On Thursday afternoon - after a long, but surprisingly comfortable flight across the Atlantic, she and Jeff sat in the departure lounge at Athens airport, waiting to board their connecting flight to Crete.

Though she'd slept through much of it, Ellie was still fatigued and more than a little tipsy from the liberally poured alcohol in the business class cabin.

Still, her chatty new colleague was great fun to spend time with (not to mention wickedly indiscreet about their famous boss) and throughout the journey she and Jeff had become firm friends.

"You know, that hottie over there has been

checking you out for the past five minutes," Jeff commented now, nodding across the departure lounge.

Ellie too had noticed a gorgeous guy throw a couple of appreciative glances her way. About early thirties, he had the look of a native, and 'hottie' was indeed an appropriate description.

But he'd obviously heard Jeff talking about him and just then quickly turned back to the book he was reading.

"And now you've scared him off," she muttered. "Great job, wingman."

Jeff shrugged. "He shouldn't be looking anyway. How does he know we're not together?"

Ellie chuckled. "Really? You honestly think we look like a couple?"

"Fair enough," Jeff said, feigning hurt.

People in the waiting area started to move about restlessly, and Ellie realised they were about to start boarding their flight.

"Where are you sitting on this one?" she asked, getting out her boarding pass. There was no business class option on the connecting flight to the island. Unfortunately.

But at least the trip was short.

"Across the aisle and one up from you, I think."

Out of the corner of her eye, Ellie saw the guy looking at her again across the waiting area. It was surprising, she thought as after such a long flight, she must look terrible.

She was wearing a pair of white jeans that emphasised her long legs and had paired it with an oversized black t-shirt that showed just the right amount of cleavage.

"Sexy without being slutty - nice," Jeff had described her upon meeting him at San Francisco airport earlier.

The hottie seemed to sense Ellie looking at him, but instead of acknowledging that she too was checking him out, he quickly went back to his book.

It was a shame because he truly was handsome as sin.

His eyes were deep brown, and though his black hair was a curly mass, it had gorgeous silkiness to it. Unlike most of their fellow travellers - mostly tourists who had dressed down for the coming flight - he was also meticulously well put together. Shiny brown shoes, dark-pressed pants, refined buttoned-up shirt with the sleeves folded up to his elbows.

She leaned over and whispered into Jeff's ear.

"Is he actually Greek or just of Greek descent do you think?"

Jeff scanned him and said, "Your observational skills are horrible. Greek, obviously."

"How do you know?"

"Other than the obvious— no tourist I've seen has ever worn anything other than sneakers on a flight— he's reading a translated Stephen King."

So he was. Ellie hadn't noticed that. And a nice coincidence that he was a King fan too.

"You should go talk to him," Jeff said. "You're probably not seated anywhere near him. It's now or never."

Ellie thought about it, but then the guy looked up at the airline stewardess as she announced boarding, and suddenly jumped up and walked away as if he'd realised he was sitting in the wrong waiting area.

Disappointed, she watched him leave.

CHAPTER SIX

*Y*awning hard as she trooped tiredly onboard, Ellie had the cold air blasting at full force and her little neck pillow wrapped around her as soon as she had stowed her carry-on bag.

She plopped down into her window seat and was asleep before the aircraft was even half-boarded.

"Wake up," she heard Jeff whisper in her ear, startling her. "Ellie!"

She snapped awake. "What? What's wrong?" she asked, groggily. "Are we landing already?"

Jeff pointed behind her. "In one minute that Greek hottie who ogled you in departures and who you in turn ogled back is going to come out of the bathroom and sit back down beside you. Try not to drool all over him this time."

Beside her?

Ellie caught sight of the Greek Stephen King book face down and open on the vacant seat alongside hers. The hot guy was actually sitting *beside* her; she must have been already asleep when he'd boarded...

"I didn't drool *that* much when I looked at him—" she argued.

"Nope, I mean *literally*." Jeff held up his phone and waggled it at her as he mouthed, "I'll show you later."

The Greek with the beautiful brown eyes was returning to his seat, and Ellie ripped her neck pillow off, shimmied her oversized top straight, and pretended to be looking out the window when he sat back down next to her.

Had she just drooled onto him in her sleep? *Please God, no.*

She discreetly glanced at his left shoulder. Oh hell ... his dark shirt was blotted all over. Not only had Ellie apparently rested on him while asleep, but she had obviously cuddled right into him to find the most comfy spot too. Mortifying!

Ignoring her, he pulled out his Greek version of *Mr. Mercedes.* Ellie looked at her watch and saw that they still had a little while to go with the journey.

May as well get this over with, she thought.

"Erm …I've just been informed that I've been sleeping on you. I'm so sorry," Ellie said to him.

He chuckled and looked up from his book. "It's OK. It's part of the flying experience. Part of … how you would say … the package."

Ellie tried to smile, but what came out was more of a grimace than anything else.

"And I've also been told I drooled on you," she admitted.

"Did you? Hm, I didn't notice."

A lie, but a white one. The best kind.

"So," she said changing the subject. "Stephen King? Do you like him?"

"Very much," he said. "I just finished the JFK one, *11/22/63.* Have you read it?"

Ellie nodded. "I try to read widely, but every time I pick up a book for travel, it's a King one." She shrugged. "You know any book by him is going to be good. Did *11/22/63* break your heart as much as it broke mine?"

The man zeroed his gaze upon her and nodded devoutly. "The whole time I was reading it, I could have cared less about Jake going after Oswald. The real story was the love story."

"I know. I wept after I finished it. He could have

been so happy. Why didn't he just stay? Why didn't he just teach?"

"I cried too," the man said.

Ellie's brain stopped. A man had just admitted to crying over a love story. The accent gave him away as not American, but admitting to crying cemented it.

"But part of it bothered me, though," she said. "So often in stories, the moral is that man should lay aside his own ambitions and be content with a simple life. Is it so wrong to want more out of life? To try and do something noteworthy? Can't you do both? Why does it have to be a choice."

"No, I don't think that's what Mr. King was saying. I think he was saying that love is just as historical as anything else. That *it is* the great thing in your life— not the other stuff you think is."

"Uh-oh, I think I'm sitting next to a romantic," Ellie joked.

"But the message is true, don't you think? It feels right. When you have true love you could not care less about everything else going on in the world. That you're not settling if you abandon your historical, grandiose notions because love is more powerful than anything you could imagine. It truly is something that deserves your complete, undivided attention, yes?"

Wow. Ellie swooned a little, wondering what kind of conversations this guy had with people he knew.

She decided then and there that she wanted to know.

"I'm Ellie. Ellie Moore." She held out her hand.

"Chris. Christos Katsaros."

They shook hands. His was strong and calloused but made a point to grip hers gently.

"So have you personally known that kind of love?" Ellie asked, not caring that it was her obvious way of asking if he had a girlfriend.

"Me? No. But I believe in it. And my parents, I believe they have it."

"That's nice."

They chatted for a little more until eventually she asked: "Are you from Crete, Chris?"

"Yes. I live in the town of Hersonnissos."

"Oh really? How strange! I'm going to Hersonnissos too."

As Ellie said this, a little voice in her head told her to back up a little and not come across as too eager or forward.

"Yes. My parents and I run a restaurant there," he continued. "It's a very popular place. Perhaps you've heard of it ..."

Ellie gasped. Cosmic synchronicity - or fate - was

something she truly believed in. Like the pounding of a prescient drum in an Alfred Hitchcock movie, it comes and you can't do a damn thing about it.

Please don't say it, she begged, unable to believe this. For the love of God don't say—

"…it's called Thasos."

CHAPTER SEVEN

*S*oon after, the plane landed at Chania International Airport. It was early morning, judging by the light.

The sun was rising amidst glowing orange clouds, and the Aegean sea appeared darker than it probably would in an hour or two. Right then it was a rippling dark purple mass.

Ellie walked off the plane behind Chris. She had steered the conversation away from the restaurant as quickly as she could, but not before he'd invited her to visit there.

What could she do but say yes? She was not only going to go - this evening actually - but she *had* to go, and Chris was going to see her when he did, thinking she was there to see him.

And he'd be right, but not completely.

In the arrivals hall, he stopped amidst the busy crowd and, fished his wallet out. He handed her a business card with his phone number, email and address of the restaurant.

"Come and eat at our place, please" Chris reiterated. "Don't worry about reservations."

"I will," Ellie said, smiling. "I'd really like that."

"I must hurry now. I got a text while I was sleeping that I needed to pick up some shipments of food on my way back. Our normal driver woke up sick. If I speed and ignore every traffic law, I won't be too late for the pickup time." He chuckled. "It is a relief. At least the place hasn't burned down in my absence."

Jeff was waiting for her in the carousel area and whipped out his phone as soon as Ellie appeared.

"I've been *dying* to catch up with you," he gasped, smiling. "I've wanted to show you these photos for so long I'm shaking in excitement."

"Go ahead," Ellie sighed. "Let's get it over with."

Jeff swiped his phone and showed her a picture of her sleeping on Chris's shoulder during the first half of the flight. Not only had Ellie found his shoulder to sleep and drool on, but she'd actually wrapped her hand around his right arm, hugging him to her.

"Oh my goodness. I'm all over him..." she said,

mouth agape. Mortified, she sheepishly asked Jeff to delete it, but not before sending a copy to her. He nodded and did so there and then.

"That's not the only one I wanted to show you, though. See, check these out. In particular, this pic." He held up a picture of Ellie with her mouth open and drool running down her chin. "It's my favourite. You look like a zombie. I'm going to airbrush some blood on you and blow it up for *Walking Dead* nights. Want me to send this one to you, too?"

It was then that Ellie realised that Jeff truly *would* be a friend for life.

He already had too much on her.

IT TOOK another couple of hours for the two to reach Hersonissos from the airport, but it was a relaxed and easy drive in a transport shuttle.

The island of Crete was a lot more hilly than Ellie had imagined. Also less green than she thought it would be, she commented to Jeff.

"That's the West Coast," her colleague whom she knew had visited before, told her. "The east coast is a lot drier for some reason. Go west and you'll feel like you're in a rainforest."

There were some trees but they were mostly variations of pine or palm, and the few shrubs that grew from the white, parched earth were dry and dwarfed-looking. They made the whole East Coast look like one long extended dune.

Ellie rolled the window of the shuttle down and noted that even the air seemed dry. A digital thermometer on the dash blinked that it was in the upper eighties, but it didn't feel like it. The old saying *it's not the heat, it's the humidity* was true.

But Hersonissos itself was bustling with people and alive with dynamic architecture packed at every turn. Brightly coloured mopeds zoomed by, people walked and talked in steady streams, and the air smelled of a combination of fried food and salty air.

The shuttle dropped them off in front of their hotel, which Jeff had chosen wisely— the Aegean Sea crashed into the sand just a stone's throw away.

They tried to check in but were informed by a gorgeous but snotty receptionist with perfect hair, perfect skin, and perfect nails that they were much too early.

Ellie begged, but to no avail. "Please. It feels like we've been travelling for days - we can't just wander around for six more hours. You have to have something. I'll take anything."

"No, this cannot be done. It is against procedure. If

you want, you may leave your bags with us until your room is ready."

"But it's not about the bags …" Ellie began.

Jeff pushed his way in and took over.

"Hey there," he said to the receptionist in a very low, deep voice. Then he leaned in, puffed his chest out, and complimented her hair before explaining that they had just been on an excruciatingly long flight with two connections, and the thought of waiting until three in the afternoon was simply inconceivable. Ignoring her weak protests to his compliments, he then idly asked what perfume she was wearing.

"It works well for you," he said, laying it on thick. "Always wear it. You smell… I can't even explain it. It's almost nostalgic for me…" He pretended to think, and said, "Oh, I know, don't take this the wrong way, but you smell just like the girl I took to my senior prom. The one who got away …"

Ellie couldn't believe that any woman would actually believe an iota of this blatant nonsense, but incredibly Jeff's flirtations were working.

Blushing deeply, the receptionist eventually took their passport details and magically 'found' a room Jeff and Ellie could use to freshen up until theirs was ready. That was if they didn't mind sharing for the moment - whereupon she looked over at Ellie as if she were some kind of fungus.

"We'll phone when your rooms are ready," she said to Jeff, who took her hand and kissed it. The girl practically swooned.

In the elevator, Ellie said, "You sure know how to lay on the charm, Romeo."

He grinned. "I know how to get what I want if that's what you're saying."

They unloaded their luggage and Jeff said he was going to go for a walk, leaving with nothing but his wallet and his sunglasses.

Ellie stripped down and took a quick hot shower. It felt great to get out of her travelling clothes. During those last couple of hours in the shuttle, it felt like her jeans were trying to meld and become one with her skin.

She cranked the water as hot as it could go and was happy to find it could go quite high. When she finished showering, she went out to the balcony overlooking a quiet beach.

She hadn't even thought to bring a swimsuit, but now wished she had. Truth be told, she didn't like how she looked in swimsuits, be they one-pieces or bikinis.

She was too tall and felt like she looked like an Amazonian warrior enough as it was. Showing a lot of skin just seemed to make it worse. But she thought she could brave it here - especially in this heat.

As it was September, the kids would likely be back in school, but the weather was still amazing.

She went in and collapsed onto the bed, thinking about meeting Chris on the plane. How typical was it that the one guy she had genuinely been attracted to in years was slated to be her first victim as Zack Rose's marketing person?

Talk about fate - not to mention bad timing.

She recalled his eyes— those beautiful, dark brown eyes— and remembered what he'd said about love.

"....more powerful than anything you could imagine. It truly is something that deserves your complete, undivided attention."

"I work for the devil," she moaned into her pillow.

Only Satan would have Ellie crush such a beautiful, sensitive man in the name of progress.

CHAPTER EIGHT

*S*he woke up mid-afternoon and realised she should get up soon if she didn't want to be jet-lagged throughout the entire trip.

She turned on the TV in the background while she got ready, and it automatically came on to a cooking program.

Of course.

There was her boss— Mr. Zack Rose himself, smiling and looking straight at her. Ellie thought his presence - albeit on TV - was more than a little eerie as if he was keeping an eye on her through the screen.

Zack was telling a story about his Greek grandfather, but that's not what she found eerie. What got to her were his eyes. The rest of him seemed jovial and animated, but not his eyes. His gaze was cold and

calculating as if communicating a different message—
one solely intended for Ellie.

*You better draw blood, they said. You are there to do my
bidding. Don't forget it.*

Ellie switched off the TV.

The sound of the ocean was better.

"I'M SO glad you're wearing heels," Jeff said to her later,
while they were waiting for their taxi to come to the
hotel. "It means you own your height which is sexy if
you embrace it. And I never would have thought it, but
white looks great on you, and it's just the right amount
of tight."

"Thanks - I think."

The taxi driver who pulled up was an overweight,
balding man badly in need of a shave. He looked back
at them once they were seated and asked, in perfect
English, where they wanted to go.

"Thasos - the restaurant? You know it?" Ellie asked,
buckling herself in.

He blinked slowly and nodded. "Yes, I know it and
can take you there. No problem. But you should know,
this time of day the traffic is unpredictable. It can be
rough, even outside of the tourist rush. If you want,

we can agree on a fixed price or we can go by time. It's up to you."

"How long in good traffic would it take us to get there?" Jeff asked.

The man shrugged. "It's hard to say. Maybe a minute or two in perfect conditions. Twenty euros, though, and I'll take you there. It doesn't matter to me. I'm working either way."

Jeff and Ellie looked at each other and silently communicated that this seemed fair. This was a work trip after all.

"OK," her colleague said. "Works for us," and handed the driver the money.

The man pocketed it and shifted his taxi to first gear.

Ellie was about to ask Jeff if he had researched anything about Thasos when the car suddenly stopped.

"There," the driver said and pointed to the restaurant. He had driven them about four blocks away from the hotel.

Jeff bit the inside of his cheek and said, "The traffic conditions. They were good then?"

"Perfect," the driver said and chuckled.

Ellie was still shaking her head in disbelief as they got out, but Jeff shrugged as the taxi drove off.

"There's one of those guys in every city on this little planet. He got us. Just count your losses and move on."

"But I didn't pay. You did," she pointed out, trying to keep a straight face. She was amazed anyone could get one over on Jeff.

"All the more reason for you to keep on walking," her colleague said through gritted teeth and took her arm as they walked up to Thasos' front of house.

Over the roaring of the ocean surf, a young man asked if they had reservations. Ellie gave him the details as Zack had already arranged and he led them inside.

The first thing the two noticed about Thasos, other than the delicious scent of Mediterranean cooking, was a pianist in the back near the patio, playing soft, melodic music.

Ellie liked it, and so did Jeff, who stared at the pianist with intense curiosity.

"I think I know him," he whispered.

"Who?" she asked, looking around.

"The piano player. I've watched him on YouTube for years now. He doesn't upload much, but on occasion he does. His mic needs to be upgraded, the video quality looks like something from the mid-nineties, there's never any description below, but..." he trailed off and Ellie inwardly laughed at him for verbalising his YouTube pet peeves.

He turned to the maitre d' and asked, "He composed the music he's playing right now, didn't he?"

"Patrick? Yes, everything he plays he composes. He comes here to try out his new music. That and he seems to like the acoustics here."

The man led them to a table in a corner that gave Jeff an uninterrupted view of the pianist.

Ellie's seat allowed her to look out at the sea. The north side of the restaurant was one big wall of panelled glass that could be opened back in high summer. Instantly transfixed by the beautiful Aegean waters, she relaxed and took in the view.

She briefly glanced into the kitchen to see if she could spy Chris, but there was no sign.

The pianist finished a song and Jeff softly clapped for him. Ellie noticed that he and the other man made eye contact for a moment before he went into another song.

Then suddenly Chris popped up beside her and her mind went blank.

"Ellie!" he exclaimed. "I'm so glad to see you again so soon." He glanced at Jeff. 'And who is this with you?"

"Don't worry, buddy - we're not together," Jeff said

without looking at him. Ellie tried to smile, but Chris seemed a little taken aback.

"He was on the flight with us," she said. "You just didn't see him. He's my colleague ... I mean friend... Jeff."

Chris seemed to think about offering his hand to shake, but reconsidered, as Jeff seemed off in his own world watching the piano player.

"So have you recovered from the flight?" Chris asked Ellie. "Are you on Crete's time zone, or San Francisco's?"

"I napped for most of the afternoon and feel a lot better now," Ellie admitted. She looked around. "So, nothing appears to have burned down anyway," she joked, recalling how he'd mentioned on the flight that he was worried the restaurant would burn down in his absence. "Unless all of this is new."

Chris laughed. "Yes, everything was fine. But I've been thinking about what you said earlier. About how everyone comes running to me because they see me as the competent one. If my parents had someone else or were forced to make decisions on their own, things might run a little more smoothly around here."

Ellie smiled, happy that he'd been thinking about her, though she still felt guilty for the brief information she'd gleaned from him about the restaurant on the flight.

"So has anyone brought you a menu yet?" he asked then.

She shook her head.

"Good. Then I will be your waiter tonight." He bowed solicitously, before going off to pick up two menus. "I will give you a moment, and then offer some recommendations if you need any, but please take your time."

Ellie thanked him and was looking down at the menu when she noticed that Jeff had since got up and was talking to the piano player.

Great. Abandoned already.

CHAPTER NINE

*S*he glanced at the menu and very quickly knew what she was going to get. She'd already familiarised herself with Thasos's offerings via her research, and there was one dish in particular she was anxious to try.

Her thoughts meandered back to Chris and how he'd been so kind and solicitous towards her, completely unaware that she was at his restaurant under false pretences.

If she hadn't gotten so lost in her thoughts she might have noticed Jeff walk away from the pianist and pull his phone out to show to Chris.

It was Chris's light laughter that broke her from her reverie.

Jeff draped a casual arm over the Greek man's

shoulders as he swiped through pictures on his phone - the ones of Ellie draped all over him on the plane.

Her face burned with mortification. She could have jumped up and tackled Jeff to the ground right then.

They walked back to the table, chuckling like two schoolboys.

"Do you need more time?" Chris asked as Jeff sat back down.

"No, I think I'm ready to order," she said through gritted teeth.

Jeff said he was too. "Can I have the grilled Psari? That's enough for me for the moment. It looks like plenty."

Chris nodded. "Good choice and it is, believe me. My mother spared nothing when she created that dish. I think she had a growing teenage boy in mind when she did. I used to eat anything I could get my hands on when I was younger."

He took Jeff's menu and then turned to Ellie. There wasn't the slightest smirk on his face as he waited and she had to marvel at his manners, given the photographs of her at her worst he'd just seen. He really was a true gentleman.

As his delicious brown eyes bored into hers, she gulped, trying to remember what she had decided to get.

"Can we start with a side of spanakopita?" she asked. "And for my main dish may I have the moussaka? And for wine, can you choose something that you think would accompany everything for both of us?"

"Of course," Chris said, smiling and taking her menu.

When he was gone, Ellie rounded on Jeff. "I can't believe you …" But he simply, shushed her, once again absorbed in the pianist's music.

Her phone vibrated with a text message. She pulled it out thinking it would be her mom or Maria checking that she'd arrived OK, but it wasn't.

Send me pictures of the food or anything else you think is useful.

Swallowing hard, Ellie surreptitiously snapped a couple of pictures of the restaurant just to show her boss that she and Jeff were there as arranged and sent them to Zack along with a message: *"Awaiting appetiser. Will send more as food arrives."*

"Do."

Feeling like a heel, she quickly put her phone away when Chris came back with a plate of spanakopita and a bottle of white wine.

"This is an Assyrtiko from the small island of

Skiathos - a beautiful place to visit if you are ever able," he said.

Jeff nodded. "I visited for a few days with my father when I was still in college. It was …" he paused and thought for words, "a very hard place to leave."

Chris uncorked the bottle and poured some for Ellie and Jeff to taste.

It was dry with bitter citrus notes. Ellie wasn't much of a wine enthusiast, but she liked it. Jeff seemed to also. Theatrically he swished the sample around in his glass and then in his mouth before drinking it.

"It's got a lot of surprises to it actually," he commented. "How much does a bottle of this typically cost?"

"In American dollars? About $300."

Ellie felt a sting of sticker shock but then remembered that it was Zack and not she who was paying for this.

"I like it," she said, breathing a sigh of relief. Chris filled both their glasses and then stood back and waited for Ellie to try the spanakopita.

Cut in hand-sized triangles, the spinach pie - a Greek speciality - felt like it was cooked perfectly. Not too soggy, not too crispy. It had a nice weight to it, too.

She took a bite and smiled. Feta cheese and butter made everything in life taste better— even spinach.

In college, she had a brief encounter with vegetarianism. For one year she fought the fight, and it was dishes like spanakopita that made it last as long as it did.

It was a small Greek restaurant a stone's throw away from her dorm that introduced her to spanakopita. She ate there at least once a week, and when she did she always got an extra spinach pie to take home. She had thought at the time that she would never find anywhere else as well able to make that particular dish.

She was wrong.

"Everything about this is perfect," she said to Chris. "The spinach isn't too dry or too wet, and the breading is simply wonderful."

"Yes, I know," he agreed with a smile. "It's my mother's recipe. I didn't know how good it was until I started eating out on my own as a teenager. It was then that I realised my parents were offering something important to the restaurant world."

"How long have they had this place?"

"My whole life," he told her. "But we just own the restaurant, not the building. This we rent. The owner was an architect my father knew. Somehow he got permission, the architect I mean, from the city to construct this building around the remains of a temple that was standing. These columns you see outside have been at this geological location for over a thousand years. The glass, the wood, and the lighting were all built around it. Everything but the stone is new. It's seamless."

"Did he know he wanted to put a restaurant here? The architect?" Ellie asked.

"Yes, and to tell you the truth, I'm quite positive he built everything with my parents in mind. I've seen pictures of him eating at our house before I was born. I think he already knew they could make something magical if he gave them the space to do it. Both my father and my mother were top-rated cooks long before this place was built."

"Sounds like he was a wise man," Jeff commented.

"*He* was," Chris said, emphasising for contrast. "His son though… " He shook his head.

There was a story there Ellie realised, but decided not to push.

At least, not unless she had to.

"Do you cook?" she asked instead.

"I do, a little - but my take on Greek food is a little different from my parents. They are more traditional whereas I'm a little more modern. One day, I hope to have my own restaurant as successful as this one. When I start it - perhaps when my parents are gone - I don't want anyone to know I was involved with Thasos. I want everyone to just like it for what it is and forget all about this place."

Interesting. Ellie realised, brightening a little. *He wants this place forgotten, too.*

Perhaps Zack had nothing to worry about after all, and Thasos would simply fade away in its own time?

She knew from her research that Chris's parents were in their late sixties, and wouldn't be able to keep this place going forever - especially if their son wasn't going to continue the family legacy.

"Your meals should almost be ready," he said. "I'll be back in a few moments."

When he was back in the kitchen, Jeff turned to her. "Some interesting information there," he said. "Did you catch it? Sounds like the place is already on a downward spiral if the guy isn't going to stick around. This might not even have to get dirty."

Ellie hoped not. For as little as she knew about Chris, she didn't want to hurt him.

The music stopped and Jeff rose again and went to talk to the piano player, who smiled this time when he saw him.

Clearly, he was making progress.

Ellie's phone buzzed once more in her pocket and she sighed.

She truly hated herself for doing so, but she sent a short message to Zack, detailing the dish she'd just eaten as well as the wine.

Family recipe. Incredible.

Zack shot back with: How do you know it's a family recipe?

Owner's son told me.

Great work! Keep talking to him!

On it :)

She wasn't one to use emoticons, but she wanted him off her back. A smiley suggested enthusiasm and energy for the task at hand.

Both things Ellie was sorely lacking just then.

She saw the top of Chris's head coming out of the kitchen and she quickly put away her phone.

"This looks even better than it normally does," he said to her and winked. "I'm not joking. I wish I could pull up a seat and share it with you."

Ellie chuckled, "You can if you want. You don't have to be formal with me."

She saw that he considered it, but he shook his head and said, "There are a few regulars in here. It would cause too much of a stir. It would get back to everyone in the kitchen and then my parents would find out. Then you'd be eating with my mother who, though smiling, would harass you to find out everything about your past, your parents' past, and what your grandparents did during World War 2."

Ellie laughed and said, "But really... it would be nice to talk with you some more. It's my first time in Crete and I'd appreciate some suggestions for places to see - from a local, especially."

Chris smiled then nodded then towards Jeff. "Well as your travelling companion seems already.... otherwise distracted, something tells me you'll be spending some of this trip on your own and we can't have that. Maybe the day after tomorrow, I can show you around a little before the restaurant opens in the evening?" he suggested.

"Sounds great." Ellie smiled and tried to convince herself that this was all in the name of more research on Zack's behalf, but she wasn't successful.

Chris was wonderful and she did want to spend more time with him.

"Where are you staying? I can pick you up," he asked.

She gave him the hotel name, deciding to not bring up the fact that she and Jeff had stupidly taken a taxi over and gotten swindled in the process.

"Perfect," Chris said. "I live close by. So did you have any particular plans? Would you like to do something early?"

"Not really. But something early is fine by me. Maybe ten?"

"I'll see you then. For now, I must leave you to your food."

Ellie looked at her moussaka: alternating layers of thinly sliced potatoes and eggplant topped off with ground beef and drowned in a creamy white bechamel-parmesan sauce.

One bite in and she nearly wept. The textures alone made her ravenous for more.

She took out her phone and snapped off another picture.

We've got our work cut out for us ...

In more ways than one.

CHAPTER TEN

*H*aving spent her first full day in Crete catching on her sleep and familiarising herself with her surroundings, Ellie woke up early, the morning Chris was due to pick her up, and decided to walk around the town a little before he arrived.

Jeff, who had spent the previous day with Patrick the pianist, was once again out and about with his new friend.

He and Ellie had decided to spend the next few days uncovering more about Chris's family situation and future plans before they told Zack anything else about Thasos, or formulated plans for a rival restaurant.

Ellie tried to tell herself that today would be part of that research, but there was no denying that she was looking forward to seeing Chris again. There was something about him, something besides his good looks, that had drawn her to him right from the very beginning.

She knew it would be a huge struggle to put her professional feelings before personal where he was concerned, but for the sake of her new job, she had no choice but to do so.

But that didn't mean she shouldn't enjoy spending time with him in the process.

On the way down in the hotel elevator, an elderly couple got in.

Speaking Russian, their voices were soft and tender to one another. Though the man stood erect and stared directly ahead (Ellie suspected because she was there), his wife couldn't stop looking at him.

She scooted close to him and reached for his hand, and he took it without hesitation. More gentle words were exchanged between them, and the wife put her head on his shoulder.

Love seemed an inadequate word for these two.

Ellie ached watching them. That gentle knowingness and stillness that came from being with someone for years; that complete faith and confidence from knowing your partner loves you and would do nothing ever to slight you; a feeling that doesn't fade, transition, or mutate, but instead escalates and deepens with each passing year.

She wanted that.

The doors opened, and the man insisted Ellie exit first.

Outside, Hersonissos was alive and bustling. People chatted as they walked along the shore. Children laughed and ran into the water. Bells on doors jingled as shops opened their doors.

Ellie noted that people made a point to look her in the eye and say good morning as she walked by.

Were they just being polite to the lonely tourist girl? Or did people here actually take notice of one another?

It was a few blocks before Ellie realised that she didn't actually know where she was going, and that she had just been walking aimlessly. Then she saw a familiar sign and recognised she was nearing Thasos from the other direction.

Fate, as it would turn out, was at work yet again.

An older woman spoke to a man just outside the entrance to the restaurant. The guy looked not much older than Chris and he was doing most of the talking.

He gestured to the woman and then back at the restaurant with quick jabs of his forefinger, spittle flying from his lips.

The woman— late sixties or even early seventies— wore a blue bandana and a long, ankle-length white dress in the traditional Greek style. Whatever she was hearing was clearly news to her.

She tried to stand tall and defiantly to mirror the confrontational man, but the weight of her heavy breasts (or maybe the gravity of the news) only allowed her to do so in short bursts— like a push toy where every push and release of the button either makes the toy stand or collapse to the ground.

As Ellie got closer, her college Greek allowed her to understand one thing the woman was saying. *Eíste o gios tou patéra sou.* "You are your father's son."

She didn't say it indignantly, though. Rather it came out as a question. *Your father's son huh? Are you and he related?*

There was no question in Ellie's mind now that this woman was Chris's mother and the man was their landlord— the son of the architect he'd spoken about the other night and toward whom he'd hinted at mixed feelings.

The conversation abruptly ended then, and the man turned from the older woman and walked the five feet back to his shiny black sports car.

When he was out of sight, the woman who Ellie guessed was Chris's mother allowed herself a sob and staggered back into the restaurant. The built-in bolt clicked home, the lights turned off, and the shades fell closed.

Ellie wanted to console her, but what would she say? What could she possibly say to a woman whose very livelihood was being threatened— not just by that man but by her boss too?

And she realised then that Thasos wasn't just a restaurant, business rival or threat to Zack Rose's world domination.

Behind it were real people, with feelings and lives at stake like Chris and his poor mother.

Now that she'd seen the place first-hand and the people behind Thasos, could Ellie truly - in all good conscience - be the architect of this lovely family's downfall?

CHAPTER ELEVEN

She made sure to be back at the hotel in time
for when Chris said he would arrive to pick
her up. She walked into the lobby and sure enough, he
was already there asking the hotel clerk to call her
room.

"I'm telling you I know her. She came to my restaurant the other night." By his tone, Ellie could tell he
wasn't making light conversation.

"We met on a flight," he continued. "Her name's
Ellie Moore. Why would I know her full name? If she
didn't want to see me, why would I know she's even
here?"

"*Pígaine stin paralía. Ypárchoun korítsia ekeí.*"

Go to the beach, there are lots of girls there. Ellie's

four semesters of Greek were about eighty per cent confident that's what the guy said.

"Hey stranger," she sang out, thinking it best to intervene before things got ugly. The normally affable Chris looked just about ready to punch his compatriot.

"Ellie!" he greeted and hugged her. "This man thinks I am trying to stalk you - at ten in the morning." He looked at the clerk who shrugged and went back to his business.

"Good to know he's trying to be protective," she joked, trying to make light of the situation.

Chris gave the man one last stare down, and then asked, "Ready?"

"Sure. So where are you taking me?"

"I thought we should go somewhere a little off the beaten track. You're here for a little while, yes? What you see here in Hersonissos is not the *real* Crete. While my home town is charming it is…" he struggled, "now much like you'd find in any other touristy area. So I thought I would take you to the west. It's a bit of a drive, but worth it." Then his eyes travelled to her clothes. "You wouldn't, by chance, have anything else you can wear would you?"

Ellie blushed hotly. "I do, but… You don't like what I'm wearing?"

He chuckled a little. "No, no, that's not what I meant. I was thinking we might go walking. Crete's known for a lot of things - mostly beaches and old ruins, but one thing tourists don't seem to know about us is that we have excellent hiking trails. The best in the world, I'm told, but I can't say for sure as it's all I know."

Ellie beamed. "Hiking?" Her father used to take her hiking in Yosemite when she was younger, but she hadn't done so in a very long time.

Chris nodded. "I thought also we could pick up some, what do you call it in America, 'brunch?' A combination breakfast and lunch. We can pick up something along the way. Like I said, though, we will be in the car for a while, but if you're visiting Crete, then one place you must go is Sfakia. I would be derelict in my duties as a native if I did not take you there. But your friend, Mr. Jeff, will he be OK without you today? He's more than welcome to come along."

"Jeff? No, he's fine. He's with the piano player from your bar. They hit it off the other night."

Chris smiled but seemed a little surprised, his face suggesting he hadn't known either man was gay.

Ellie went up to her room and changed out of her skirt into shorts and a light t-shirt before heading back down.

Chris smiled appreciatively at her long toned legs. "So, let's have an adventure."

"Let's," Ellie replied, smiling back.

CHAPTER TWELVE

Walking around town earlier, most of the cars she had seen were small, energy-efficient Hondas, or cute little Fiats.

Growing up, Fiats reminded Ellie of clown cars at the circus and with her height she couldn't imagine fitting in one, let alone driving one. People had cars of all sizes back in the US, but tiny cars seemed in absolute abundance on Crete.

So when Chris walked her back to an old, rusty-looking farm truck, she was a little taken aback, but pleasantly so. Here was a vehicle that wouldn't ensure her knees ended up in her eye sockets in case of a collision.

Chris unlocked the door and held hers open for her. No one in America had ever held open a door for

Ellie, and it seemed fitting that the first one to do so would be the proud Greek owner of a beat-up old Chevy.

With a roar and one big plume of black smoke upon starting, Chris eventually got them up to cruising speed before heading westbound on Crete's northern coast.

The truck's elongated bench seating was comfy enough, but the seams were undone in many spots and leaking yellow foam.

The steering wheel was a faded robin-egg's blue and was so large that Chris barely had to turn it to take them into a hard turn.

He used this ability on many occasions when cars drifted into his lane. No one in Crete seemed to check their mirrors before merging; it was an unspoken rule that Chris be forced to yield to any and all incoming traffic.

Unlike Ellie, if she had been at the wheel, Chris was calm and unperturbed by everyone's seemingly senseless driving.

They chatted and listened to the radio as they drove. It was an old, metallic one with manual tuning and volume dials. Ellie didn't know what they were listening to, but it sounded like music to a film. When she asked Chris if he knew, he said he thought it was the soundtrack to *The Thin Red Line*.

"Sounds like Hans Zimmer," he said. "I've never seen it, but I've heard the soundtrack a couple of times."

"Are you talking about that war movie from the nineties?" Ellie asked.

"Yes. We have a soundtrack station on the island. This is one thing that surprised me when I travelled to your country. You don't have movie soundtrack stations. So much energy and enthusiasm for your movies yet where's the radio station to support that?"

Ellie had never thought about it that way.

They drove along the coast for the remainder of the morning. The truck sputtered and shook violently along the dashboard whenever Chris had to speed up, but it was otherwise a smooth journey.

Rolling treeless rocky mountains became visible at one point, and Ellie asked if there had been a recent fire.

"No, we call them the Lefka Ori, the White Mountains. Others call them the Madares, which translates to the Bald Mountains. Most of the year they are white with snow. The rest of the time, the sun shines so bright on the limestone, that they still appear white. We're going to drive between them in a little bit and head over to Sfakia soon— it's on the southwest coast of the island. Are you hungry?"

"Yes," Ellie replied, playfully scolding him. "It's a good thing I had a bagel before you arrived."

Chris cringed. "Sorry. I'm not good with time. I hope you're not starving. But there is a small restaurant on the way that if you can make it, I think you'll appreciate."

"Why is that?" she asked.

"You seemed to appreciate our food the other night. The dishes I want to get for you there is - how do Americans put it - in the same ballpark."

Ellie said that sounded good.

"I'm so sorry again. Of course, I should have fed you by now. I just... I don't know, I suppose wanted to make sure I gave you a good tourist experience."

"It's OK. Really. I'm having fun and to be honest, I haven't really thought about food since we hit the road."

It was true. It was easy to ignore hunger pains while bouncing along the countryside and seeing so many new sites. By and large, Hersonnissos had given her the impression that Crete was your standard Mediterranean tourist haunt, but that wasn't even remotely the case. While certainly touristy, away from the coast the island was also wild and largely unsettled.

The truck suddenly bucked and started to slow.

Chris cursed.

She looked at him and asked, "What's wrong? Are we breaking down?" Her earlier fear had come to pass after all.

"No, no. I just … forgot to fill it up before we headed out. We're out of fuel before I thought we would be. Don't worry, I have some tanks in the back." He eased the truck over to the side of the road and turned it off.

"How much do you have?" Ellie asked anxiously as he got out. "Will it be enough?"

Chris nodded back to her. "Oh, I have plenty. I use leftover grease from the restaurant to make biodiesel."

She didn't know this could be done and said as much.

"One of the perks of running a restaurant. You have most of the ingredients to make your own gas. And you can make some for your car, too," he joked.

She giggled. He had such a cheesy sense of humour which only added to his charm.

Chris poured in several large gas tanks' worth of fuel and got back in.

Ellie had her doubts that the truck would start

back up, but it roared right to life and they were quickly cruising down the road again.

"You have lots of surprises in store, don't you?" she said looking sideways at him.

Chris winked at her. "You have no idea."

CHAPTER THIRTEEN

*A*bout an hour down the road, Ellie's stomach started rumbling. She didn't think she would be able to make it much further without eating, and admitted as much to Chris when she stopped seeing any signs of buildings or homes.

"Well this is good," he said, and turned left onto a straight and long highway that went between the White Mountains, "because we're just at where I wanted to bring you."

Though the mountains that rose high into the air were bare, the valley they were driving through was wild and abundant with life.

Sounds of chirping grasshoppers, frogs, and birds filled the truck's cab.

Chris turned off the radio so they could hear better. "We're a little more than halfway to the trail. We'll fuel ourselves up, ride a little further, and then have a nice little walk."

The front of the truck dropped down when the road ceased being paved. Behind them, waves of dust swirled into an opaque cloud.

"It's a lot different on this side of the island, isn't it?" he said to Ellie. "Almost feels like a different planet. Crete still surprises me, and I've lived here my whole life."

Chris slowed and pulled into a small gravelled parking area where a few Jeeps and Hondas sat. He turned the engine off and pointed to a trail that went into the forest.

"The restaurant is through there," he said.

"Is it also a monastery?" Ellie asked, taken aback.

"No," Chris replied. "But the people running it will make you question."

They got out and Chris held out his hand. She took it automatically, as if it was the most natural thing in the world, causing Ellie to remember the old Russian couple back at the hotel.

Chris caught her eye and when she smiled shyly, he squeezed her hand.

Oh God, I think I'm already falling for this guy...

Was he like this with all tourists though, Ellie warned herself. She knew that Mediterranean men had a reputation for being charming but feckless, so perhaps she should be on her guard, but she'd met her fair share of players back home too.

Chris seemed ... different.

"In English, the restaurant would be called *New Valley*— Néa Koiláda in Greek. You won't find it in any travel guide. Not because the owners don't want foreigners inside, but because they have no interest in advertising themselves. They are happy with the money it makes through simple word of mouth."

"Not trying to take over the world or build any franchises?" Ellie replied dubiously.

Chris nodded. "Exactly."

They crossed into the shadow of the mountain, where the air was cool and moist. Large, heavy stones bubbled up from the earth, making it necessary to watch their footsteps.

"I don't feel like we're walking to a restaurant," Ellie said. "I still feel like you're taking me to a church. I like you and all, but I don't think we're quite at that stage just yet ..." she chuckled.

"It's just up ahead," Chris assured her, smiling.

Ellie checked to see that her phone was in her pocket just in case Jeff - or worse Zack - thought to check on her. It was, but she doubted it mattered— no one got any service in places like this. Not now nor in fifty years.

Some places were just removed from the world.

And that was a good thing.

A young couple walked by and Ellie almost breathed a sigh of relief because it meant they were going somewhere. Both greeted them in Greek and passed on, moving nimbly across the rocky path as if they had walked it a hundred times.

To the right, the ground quickly rose, and trees disappeared only to be replaced by solid rock.

A babbling brook flowed to the left, and the rock closed in around them in a gorge so tight Ellie looked up to see that they weren't walking in a well-lit cave.

Just as she was about to feel claustrophobic, the tunnel widened and opened out into a clearing. A dozen or more tables (some wooden, some stone), stretched across dark green grass. It looked more like a barbecue gathering in a park than a restaurant.

Chris sat down at a polished stone table encircled by milk crates for seating.

Ellie sat across from him, looking around at the 'restaurant' in both amusement and awe.

A woman draped in black cloth placed a small candle

between them, and rather than light it with a match, went inside a nearby stone hut (where Ellie assumed they cooked the food) and came out with a candle already lit.

Holding this, she bent and lit their candle, then exited without saying a word.

Chris grinned at Ellie. He looked like a schoolboy waiting anxiously for a prank to commence.

"Are we going to get menus?" she whispered, leaning forward.

Chris shook his head. "No, they serve you what they want to serve you."

Another woman, this one older than the first, came out holding a tray with four glasses on it— two large and two small— and placed them on their table one at a time.

"The big one's obviously water," Ellie said. "What's the other one?"

"What does it smell like to you?"

Ellie brought the smaller glass to her nose and sniffed it. It didn't have a strong smell. Slightly nutty, maybe a hint of something sweet like honey, but it was otherwise bland...

She took a sip, and her throat and mouth were instantly lit with fire. She coughed and put the drink down.

"What is this? Moonshine?" she asked, wiping her eyes.

Chris looked at her confused. "Moonshine?"

"Moonshine. You know, white lightning, bootleg, Mountain Dew." Chris's vacant stare stayed locked in place. "Let me put it another way, if I had a barrel of it, and I sat on it and lit it with a match, would it get me to the moon?"

Chris's eyes widened and he erupted into laughter. His whole body laughed hard. Then he calmed and nodded, wiping away tears from his eyes. "It's alcohol if that is what you're asking me."

"What is it called?"

"Tsikoudia. Another word is Raki. Translates roughly to firewater. Is this your first time drinking it?"

Ellie said it was and took another sip. This time she almost coughed herself hoarse.

"The proof ranges anywhere from forty per cent to sixty per cent, so take it slow. I'm surprised you haven't had it yet, though I suppose this is only your second day here. Everyone on this island drinks it like water. A lot of the old locals think it's a cure-all medicine— some even put it on skin rashes and warts. I don't know about its medicinal properties, but I do know it will get you drunk. It's very good at that."

"So you brought me here to get me drunk?" she teased.

Chris picked up her hand and kissed it. "No, I brought you here to spend time with you," he said, as inwardly Ellie melted. "The firewater is just an added bonus."

CHAPTER FOURTEEN

"So they're really not going to let us pick our food?" Ellie just couldn't wrap her brain around that.

"No," Chris said smiling. "A lot of fine dining doesn't allow you to either."

Then he leaned forward towards her on the table and whispered, "Let me tell you a secret. This whole place is mine actually but nobody knows it - not even my parents. Don't tell anyone."

Her eyes widened. "Really?"

"Yes. The land is in my family's name. It's not exactly legal what we're doing here— hence the lack of advertising, and it's not going to be in existence long. It's just an experiment for me to try out various foods and a new concept should I ever start my own place."

Ellie was amazed. "How long has it been around, and how much longer will you run it?"

"There are a few more dishes I want to try out, so maybe another month. This is the only season it's been open. My friend runs it for me. We opened it at the tail end of winter around March. My friend is a great cook, but every meal I design."

The older waitress came back and set them each down a bowl of steamed leafy greens, and a small communal dish full of baked pastries.

"What is all of this then?" Ellie asked, excited.

"The main dish is *horta vrasta,* and the pastries are meat and cheese pies called kreatopitas. The horta vrasta is a vitamin powerhouse. Normally it's made from collard greens, but we've made it out of wild greens that aren't farmed anywhere. Made with collard greens, horta vrasta is great for you to eat, but since we make it from foraged greens, the nutritional value of it has multiplied tenfold."

Ellie took a big bite. The greens were similar to spinach but had a peppery bitterness to them that she liked. Chris had mollified their taste with what tasted like beet juice. She asked if she was right.

"Yes and no. It's a cousin of beets that's not farmed anywhere. It too, is foraged." He took a bite and added with a mouthful of food, "You can eat the greens on their own, but I like to pair them with the meat pies."

"Are those foraged for, too?" she asked jokingly.

"Yes. How do you describe it? Roadkill."

Ellie spit out her first bite and Chris reached across and grabbed her wrist grinning widely. "I'm joking. The meat comes from locally raised goats."

The meat pies were juicy and thick, each containing pockets of cheese that came from grass-fed cows. As they ate, Chris also informed her that everything was cooked in locally churned butter.

"One thing civilisation has forgotten," he said, "and I include America in this, is just how nutritious and healthy animal fats are for us. People didn't get sick as often as they do now. Pollution's not helping, but it's not the main culprit. How we eat is. It's why I cook with the ingredients that I do. Many of the ingredients before us are not cheap for me to obtain, and some are downright expensive. But I believe very strongly in it. Whole milk would go perfectly with this meal, but I included the firewater with it so it would detox the system. With the fresh food that's now flooding your system, you should feel wonderful by the time we get to the trail."

"Could you afford to do this in a proper restaurant setting, though?" Ellie asked, chewing.

"Of course, the profit margins would be much smaller," Chris agreed. "But I'm OK with that."

She then remembered his mother crying outside Thasos earlier after talking with the landlord, who obviously wanted more money.

In the world of fine dining, Chris's family restaurant was as successful as any, but a dramatic spike in rent could do it under as easily as it would any other business.

Profit margins had to be high for any such business to survive, and as Thasos' manager, Chris surely knew this. He should know better than anyone that daily upkeep alone ate into most restaurant's profits.

And what kind of cold-hearted landlord would raise the rent right after peak tourist season?

But since it was none of her business, she decided not to talk to Chris about what she'd seen that morning.

"Everything goes so well together," she said, forking some greens onto her pie. "This is the best meal I've had in a long time if you don't count dinner last night. I almost feel like my blood is energised."

Chris smiled warmly at the compliment. "And it will feel that way for a good while yet."

The pile of pies before them dwindled until they

were gone, long finished before they could even grow cold.

Now overly full, Ellie tried to remain ladylike and attractive while also stretching her stomach out and giving it more room.

She had a feeling she was failing miserably.

he ride to Sfakia seemed to take far less than two hours. Chris's meal had indeed energised Ellie.

Legs wrapped under her, she asked him to change the radio channel as they bounced along the dirt road and give her something to sing to.

Loud and out of tune, she sang along even though she had no idea what anyone was saying, serenading Chris directly into his ear.

He wasn't a carefree singer like her but chuckled uncontrollably as she tried to not only hit notes she'd never hit but tried to sing in a language she didn't know.

Much like back in the restaurant when he'd kissed

her hand, he surprised her again when he gently rested a strong hand on her knee between gear changes.

Forward, she thought but made sure he knew she didn't mind by scooting as close to him as she could, trying to convey to him that his touch certainly didn't offend her.

Soon he got bolder and left his hand upon her longer and longer— or at least as long as the truck would allow. It sputtered up a hill once, and Ellie wondered if it wasn't the steep climb that was causing the old truck to struggle but rather Chris's neglectful driving.

She hoped the latter, even though the truck sounded like a dying elephant.

The southern coast of Crete finally came into view at the top of one such hill. Far below, long, white beaches spread before the waters. Wispy palm trees dotted the sands and towered over the few post-summer stragglers.

"I liked the beach in Hersonnissos, but this one looks more unspoiled," she said.

"They're very different, but yes. It's roomier and there are not very many tourists out and about. Plenty of people still come, but it's a lot different from July and August."

Street parking was abundant there, also unlike

Hersonnissos, but Chris had a specific place in mind and kept driving until he pulled into an area about fifty metres from a mostly intact ruin.

It didn't have that typical ancient Greek look to it, as the stone walls were still standing, and the thatched roof was still together save for a few spots, but it looked very old.

"Late eighteenth century," Chris told Ellie once they got out. "It's been cared for off and on over the years. It was used as a supply house during Nazi occupation. If the Germans had known about it, they would have surely destroyed it. As much as they respected our people, they never hesitated to lay waste to a lot of our monuments, despite what you may have read."

"I never would have suspected people were still recovering from World War Two here," Ellie said.

"Not so much my generation, but my parents'. They have a lot of stories they still tell. Their parents burned it into them, and they, in turn, feel a need to burn it into us."

It was hard to imagine Crete as a militarised zone. Probably even harder for its citizens.

The greenery that had been at Chris's experimental restaurant was still present here, only in Sfakia wildflowers grew on almost every square foot.

The forceful winds allowed trees to grow only sparingly, so grass and flowers ruled. The breeze that pulsed incessantly off the water shook and caressed the fields of green in great, unceasing, temperamental waves.

It was a warm day, but it didn't feel it out in the wind.

Chris pointed to a stone paved path that went uphill and back north from whence they came.

"This way," he said.

Ellie's heart sank a little bit. She would like to have stayed by the ocean. Everything was so still and quiet, yet loud and moving.

Sensing her hesitation, Chris turned back and said, "It's worth it. We'll be back. Have to if we want to drive home later."

The White Mountains rose like Titans just before the shore and Ellie gasped. Did Chris honestly think she was going to climb to the top of those?

From the looks of where they were headed, yes he did.

Firs, junipers, and spruces muted the ocean once they had walked for a few minutes.

With the trees blocking the coastal breeze, the air warmed up quickly. The trail was as unforgiving as any Ellie had hiked before. Mostly uphill, she lost her breath after just a few minutes.

As a San Francisco native, she had walked up her share of hills over the years, but this one was having its say over her. She leaned forward and pushed off her knees with her hands as she walked— a walk her father would call Neanderthal.

She could only envy Chris as he walked casually upwards ahead of her.

"You have some… interesting viewpoints on how a first date should go," she tried to say after they had walked well past the parking area, but what came out sounded like a series of heavy breaths.

Chris cocked his head. "Do you need a break?" he asked.

She waved him on and he resumed walking.

The ground eventually levelled off and they reached an area devoid of trees. Rough, bare rock rose like a tower still beside them, but they were high enough in the air that they could see rocky islands far on the horizon that they couldn't see at ground level.

"Is this where you wanted to bring me?" Ellie asked, admiringly. "It's beautiful."

"Not quite," Chris said. "Still higher." He pointed at the rock and walked up its steep embankment. It looked like he planned for them to just grab a ledge and climb.

"Chris, I'm honoured you think I can do that, but seriously... I'm no rock climber."

He turned back and looked forward a few times before realising the problem. Then he moved to the side and pointed.

Just a couple of steps past him was a break in the rock. Much like the monolith from *2001: A Space Odyssey*, it looked like an alien, foreign object on an otherwise predictable terrain— an open, straight black wound cracked into unblemished solid stone.

"It's a lot easier once you make it here," Chris said, emphasising the remaining five feet Ellie had to walk to get to him. "But it will be scarier in a few minutes if you don't like heights. You're not afraid of heights, are you?"

"I don't know..." she mumbled hesitantly. "What kind of heights are we talking about?"

"The kind you never forget," he replied, with a boyish grin.

Ellie's heart fluttered automatically. With that look in his eyes, how could she resist?

CHAPTER SIXTEEN

"OK," she said and pushed forward. "Lucky for you my father scared my fear of heights out of me a long time ago."

Chris offered her his hand and pulled her up the remaining slope.

Inside the tunnel, a stream of air gushed hard and then calmed once they were a few feet in. Moss and pockets of weeds tried to grow on what little soil had snuck inside the opening, but farther in and away from the sun the path became too rocky and dark for anything to survive.

The only light came from a lightning-bolt-shaped sliver of sky above them. Ellie could see and didn't feel in any danger, but she only felt comfortable walking forward because Chris was directly in front of her.

Without him there, she'd be scooting and sliding her feet just in case the ground dropped away.

Eventually, they came to a thick steel ladder bolted into the mountain. It went up high and far.

"Ready?" Chris asked. "You're sure you're not afraid of heights?"

"Lead on, cowboy," Ellie said. "I want to see where this goes."

Smiling, he started climbing up the steel ladder one rung at a time. Then he looked back down at her and said casually as the wind, "I like you very much, Ellie. You're a lot of fun," and resumed climbing.

She blushed as she followed him, unused to such direct flirtation. But with Chris, almost right from the very beginning, it had felt right.

The ladder was bolted into the mountain about every five feet or so, and its rungs were thick and perforated to prevent slipping. It was as safe and sturdy as it could be, but Ellie still felt crazy for climbing it.

Heart pounding, she followed after Chris, not bothering to talk or continue their light banter. Only the *ting-tang-ting* of their hands and feet slapping and pressing against metal filled the air between them.

Hand over hand, step after step, up, up, and farther up they climbed out of the shadow of the mountain and back into clear, white light, though they were still wrapped around the stone's cavernous wound.

They were so high now that Ellie wouldn't allow herself to look down. With sweaty hands and a nervous heart, add one more variable and it might all be over for her.

As her father used to say, looking down was a lot of people's last bad decision. "Wait until you're safe and sound at the top to do it if you feel like you have to," he said once while they were hiking up Half Dome. "At the very least, wait for a lull, because it's one thing to know, *but it's another thing to see.*"

They reached the top where some kind soul had continued steel handles and footholds on the ledge to make it easier to climb up and down. That was the hardest part about climbing— getting up and down from the top.

Ellie crawled to a stand, where she willed herself to look down, and was immediately glad she had followed her father's advice.

The bottom was only a small circle of darkness down below.

Yet they still had further to climb. The mountain still encircling them, Chris had walked over to the next ladder and was already a few rungs up waiting for her.

"Good?" he asked.

Ellie nodded. "How many more of these are there?"

"This is the last one. But it's taller than the others. If your hands are sweaty, I recommend getting them gritty on the ground before coming up. We're going to be on this one for a while."

Ellie rubbed her hands on the sooty ground and resumed following him.

Up, up, still further up. Both were still silent as they climbed.

What struck Ellie as wonderfully divine about where they were was the utter remoteness of it. The sounds of civilisation were long gone. No people sounds, no car sounds. The only thing she could hear apart from their climbing, was the steady rush of wind at the very top, and it was howling like a wolf.

"Are you ready to be on top of the world?" Chris asked, looking down.

"As I'll ever be," she answered, breathless.

"You're brave. There are many Cretans who have never done this. The first time I did this, I was with a group of five or six friends, and the only other person to do it with me was my friend Gregor— the one running the restaurant we went to this afternoon— and he complained the entire way."

"Well, this isn't my first rodeo," Ellie said, "and what's not to like? This is beautiful!"

Chris paused and looked down. "There are thousands of places like this all over Crete, Ellie." He shrugged as if it weren't a big deal and added, "And if you'd let me, I wouldn't mind showing them to you."

Ellie met his gaze, realising that she wanted that too. She wanted to spend more time with this lovely Greek man who bit by bit was stealing her heart. They barely knew each other, but she and Chris had an intrinsic connection. It was undeniable. They both knew it.

Then Ellie suddenly remembered that whatever about Chris stealing her heart, she was here to essentially steal his livelihood, and the very thought made her stomach grow heavy.

CHAPTER SEVENTEEN

"You're just about there," Chris shouted down then. He grunted and pulled himself up.

Ellie looked up and saw he was out of sight.

She got to the top where Chris was waiting with his hand out. She took it and pulled herself free of the vacuum below her.

The light was almost blinding it was so bright. Her eyes adjusted, and suddenly all of Crete came into view. 360 degrees of it.

Ellie turned in slow circles, in utter awe at the beauty before her.

Chris chuckled knowingly and went and sat down to stare across the Aegean Sea. Blue waters were visible to the north, west and south, but to the east were green farmlands, brown chateaus, tiny white herds of sheep, and golden ribbons of road snaking in and out of view green, rolling hills.

Back to the sea, red, blue, and yellow sails pulled white dinghies across the cerulean waters.

It was overwhelmingly beautiful.

"My father's father ran away from home when he was a teenager and spent a week camped out on top of this rock," Chris said. "He'd go down just long enough to fish, catch a few tuna, and climb back up. The whole town looked for him. My great-grandfather just happened to remember the look of awe on his face when he had brought him here as a young boy and decided to check it on a whim. My grandfather wasn't here when he arrived, but something told my great-grandfather to just wait. To just be still."

"Is this the grandfather who lived in the house we saw this afternoon?" Ellie asked, sitting down beside him. "The one you're using as your experimental restaurant?"

"Yes, the very same," Chris said. "My grandfather climbed up that ladder we just finished climbing, two fish slung over his back, and when he saw my great grandfather, he didn't run. He went and sat down beside him as we are now. The two cooked the fish together in silence. And when they had finished eating, they went back home."

"Did he do it just to see the views? Why'd he leave?"

"He wasn't that young. Germany had started assisting Italy in its assault on mainland Greece. Everyone knew Crete was next, including my grandfather. When it happened, he knew he was going to have to fight for his people. This was his calm before the storm."

"There's so much history everywhere here," Ellie whispered, still in awe.

Chris nodded. "And now I am on *my* calm before the storm, Ellie. My parents don't know it yet, but Thasos will go out of business soon. The landlord I told you about has been harassing us for months. He means to shut us down soon, which is why I've been experimenting with the other restaurant and doing so much research."

Her heart ached for him, and because it seemed this landlord was doing Zack Rose's - (and indeed her) job for him, she almost came clean.

Almost.

But still, Ellie couldn't bring herself to tell Chris the real reason she'd come to Crete.

Not yet.

Maybe never.

Instead, she sat with him and looked out at the waters, hugging her knees, her secret safe within.

"Thank you for using one of those days to be with me," she said, feeling sad for him. "Time must be precious to you right now."

"All the more since I met you," Chris said. He didn't say it looking at her. "You're something special."

He didn't say it after letting the air hang still between them. He said it matter of factly while looking out at the ocean.

And that made it even worse.

CHAPTER EIGHTEEN

*a*fterwards, Chris took her to a restaurant in Sfakia that was right on the harbour. The little fishing village seemed sleepy compared to Hersonnissos, but not in a boring way.

Each town had its own heartbeat. Hersonnissos' beat was like that of someone walking excitedly to an adventure, whereas Sfakia's was like that of an old man sitting down for some meditation in his garden.

As an appetiser, Chris ordered them a simple portion of garlic bread. It was some of the tastiest bread Ellie had ever eaten. Crispy, but with pockets of warm butter that hadn't burned away, chewy but soft, and the garlic seasoning was mixed in with a sprinkling of parmesan cheese.

"This bread is made out of kamut grain, which is one that many gluten-intolerant people can tolerate."

"How so?" Ellie asked, through a mouthful of bread.

"It's an ancient grain, untouched by any modifications. The stomach can handle it because it's still how grains are supposed to be. The pasta we make at Thasos is made out of either einkorn or kamut. Gluten-sensitive people often ignore their diet while on holiday and eat whatever they want, regardless of whether or not they get hives or stomach aches. Many come to me the next day and ask me why nothing happened to them the night before."

"That could be a game changer for a lot of people, Chris. Do you advertise that? Have you bothered spreading that information around?"

He shook his head. "No. Many people in Greece know this. It's no secret to us, and wouldn't make me unique."

They ordered lamb gyros as their main dish, making sure to get two bowls of tzatziki to accompany it.

"As far as traditional food, gyros aren't high on my list. But here their tzatziki sauce is the best I've ever had, and tzatziki goes best with gyros. I've been trying to weasel the ingredients out of them for ages now, but they won't tell me. At four hours away, all I can do is insist I'm not competition, but they won't budge."

The gyros were massive (requiring two hands to lift), and the meat was cut to the perfect size. Dipped in the tzatziki yoghurt dip, Ellie abandoned all hopes of eating like a lady. She let her hands and face get covered with food, not bothering to use a napkin every time she got messy.

It hit the perfect spot after hiking all day.

They didn't get back to Hersonnissos until ten o'clock that night. Ellie fell asleep quickly after getting into his truck, but this time she purposefully found his shoulder to sleep on.

Her conscious and subconscious were now in full agreement that Chris was a wonderful guy.

If only there was a way to help him.

LATER, collapsed in bed at her hotel room, sure she was about to sleep the soundest sleep of her life, Ellie's phone chirped with a text message from Zack Rose: *"Update...?"* He'd even added an ellipsis, indicating his impatience.

She considered pretending she was asleep but decided to get it over with: "Spent the whole day with the manager. Honestly, all you need to do is wait. Landlord raised the rent so high it seems they have no hope of staying open. He expects to be out of business within a month or two."

"Shame. Any other insights into their success so far?"

Ellie's eyes widened at her boss's reply. No surprise or confusion? Just a simple 'shame'?

"Truly, there's no secret that will help you, Zack. It's a terrific location, and the parent's love of cooking is palpable. You can feel it when you walk in. The food is delicious, but it's not the food that makes it great. It's the environment."

"You can 'feel it' when you walk in? Have you been sampling the local firewater? I need something concrete, Ellie."

"Sorry, it's all I have— but I'm positive there's no better answer. It's just a good place run by good people."

Especially Chris, she thought.

Zack must not have cared for what she said, because he replied, "Where's Jeff? He seems MIA."

And he will be for quite a while, Ellie thought. He's fallen for a native, just like I have.

But of course, she didn't admit this to her boss.

Then all of a sudden a thought came to Ellie and she decided to just jump straight into her suspicion: "Are YOU behind the sudden rise in rent? Maybe the one pushing the landlord to get them out?"

No hesitation from him this time. "Guilty."

Unbelievable....

Ellie gritted her teeth and shook her head.

*"This is why I hired you, Ellie. I knew you'd be able to see through things. Keep using those eyes of yours. And awesome job cosying up to the son by the way. Never knew you had **that** in you."*

Ellie almost responded back with a sharp retort but fought the urge. Zack was her boss after all.

But she was annoyed, not because of what he had just implied, but because of his additional subterfuge and admission about the landlord.

It dispersed a lot of confusion though. The likelihood Thasos was the target of two forces out to get it after operating in Crete peacefully for thirty years without any issues hadn't quite added up.

She was so angry she could spit. What Zack was doing behind the scenes was downright low.

If Ellie hadn't spent all day hiking, she might stay up all night boiling in her anger, but her body laughed at the thought of staying awake.

So she threw her phone on the nightstand, her boss's insulting text remaining as the last communication between them.

CHAPTER NINETEEN

*S*he slept well into mid-morning, and when she awoke she immediately wanted to talk to Chris. To tell him she had had a wonderful time hiking and talking with him, and that the entire day spent together had simply felt magical.

But she didn't want to call him because he was probably already busy at the restaurant getting supplies ready for the evening.

Instead, she sent him a text message:

Thank you for yesterday. You showed me another world.

Too cheesy? Too clingy? She didn't care. He needed to know that he was on her mind. Continuously.

He wrote straight back.

"No, thank you. Thanks for listening to my crazy ideas

and maudlin rants. I was afraid I was too much of a downer last night after I talked about the restaurant...

So let me make it up to you tonight. I usually eat dinner before the crowds come in. Would you like to come to us for an early dinner today? 4:30?"

"*Love to,*" was all she wrote back.

Ellie could only hope Chris was grinning as much as she was right then.

SHE MET Chris's parents on her arrival at Thasos that afternoon.

Their English wasn't great, but Ellie was able to communicate to them that they had a really great son and that they could cook amazing food.

The father was delighted to hear this, but the mother seemed unsure, continuing to stare at Ellie as if she'd said something insulting.

She kept asking her why she was in Crete, and nothing Ellie told her seemed to satisfy her.

Annoyed, the older woman eventually left and went back to the kitchen.

Chris's father stayed around though, and asked Ellie if she'd enjoyed the hike the day before.

"It was breathtaking," she said.

In very bad English, he then began to tell the same story Chris had told her about his grandfather.

She didn't have the heart to tell him she had already heard it but noticed that Chris stopped doing what he was doing to listen too. He listened and asked questions as if it were the first time he had heard it.

Ellie could see he loved and respected his dad.

When his father was finished, Chris asked, "Ellie, do you have your phone on you? Can you show my father that funny picture Jeff took of us on the plane? He would love it."

Blushing, Ellie did so, and he and his father burst out laughing, Chris laughing just as hard as the first time he'd seen it.

"Your mother and I don't even sleep that snugly together," Chris's father joked in broken English. "I'll arrange the wedding tomorrow. You two are meant to be together!" He slapped Ellie and Chris on the back and she blushed while Chris grinned.

"Mother should see it, too," he said to Ellie and took off to the kitchen with her phone. She didn't argue. The older woman didn't seem to like her much, so maybe the embarrassing picture would help endear her to her.

Just then Jeff and Patrick the piano player came in.

"Have you heard from Zack?" she asked her

colleague in a low voice. "He says you haven't been answering his texts."

Before Jeff could reply, Chris's mother howled in the other room. She sounded as if a loved one had just died in front of her.

Alarmed, her husband ran to the kitchen door, but she pushed it open and pointed a finger at Ellie and Jeff.

"Zoýfia. Arouraíous sto spíti mou! Ádeia! Vges éxo tóra! Tha sas katára méchri to kókalo. Ádeia!"

Vermin. Rats in my house! Leave! Get out now! I will curse you down to the bone. Leave!

It was amazing how much college Greek flooded into Ellie's brain just then. She wanted to run to the old woman and ask her what was wrong, but Jeff gripped her arm and kept her from moving.

Chris came out of the kitchen next, his skin pale. He looked like he might either vomit or punch a hole through the wall.

"Ti symvaínei me ólous?" Chris's father asked. *What's wrong with everyone?*

"Chris, please tell me what's the matter," Ellie pleaded, astonished at the look on his face.

Chris staggered over to her and placed her phone back in her hand. "I shouldn't have read this. It's none of my business— you have, after all, been nothing but nice to me. But I accidentally clicked out of the picture sent by your friend. And I couldn't find his message again. But I found another. One where you and someone by the name of Zack Rose, who I can only assume is *the* Zack Rose, were discussing how my family's restaurant is being pushed out of business. He asked for insights, you sent him pictures of our food, he admitted to paying our landlord money to make us leave. I... you're an amazing actor, Ellie. I thought what we had was real. You've been lying to me since the very beginning? What is it you do, anyway?"

She swallowed hard. "I'm Zack Rose's employee," she admitted, shame filling her.

Then Chris turned to Jeff and whispered, "And you?"

He shifted and said, "Same."

Chris nodded, then went and sat down. "Please do as my mother said," he whispered, ashen. "Please leave, and don't ever come back."

CHAPTER TWENTY

*E*llie had never cried harder in all her life.

The worst part about it all was that after what she'd learned the night before, she had already decided *not* to help Zack anymore.

She didn't know how she was going to work around it, but if she had to, she'd decided she was going to quit her job if he insisted on her being part of Thasos' downfall.

He wasn't playing fair and this wasn't right.

Jeff sat in the hotel room with her, looking out over the Aegean Sea as she tried to get control over herself.

Autumn rain pelted against the balcony doors.

"What do we do, Jeff? I feel so terrible…"

Jeff turned to her and said, "Nothing in life is easy,

Ellie. Especially the good stuff. Patrick is upset with me too. I don't know how I'm going to get him back, but I'm going to because I know this: he is worth fighting for. What we need to ask ourselves is would Chris or Patrick fight for us if the roles were reversed? Patrick would. We've only known each other for a few days, but I know he would fight for me. Ellie, do you think Chris would fight for you if he was in your shoes?"

She didn't have to think about it. Those beautiful brown eyes didn't look at her like she was just some girl. They looked at her with something far deeper— something that often took a lifetime to develop.

"So let's fight this, Ellie - let's fight *Zack*," Jeff continued passionately. "We'll make sure Thasos is around this time next year. And the year after that too. Instead of being its assassins, let's become its guardian angels."

"But where do we start? What do we do?"

"I don't know yet - all I *do* know it's the only way out of this. *But*," Jeff added determination in his eyes, "'we're marketeers, remember? We'll figure it out."

CHAPTER TWENTY-ONE

"*A*dditional foot traffic isn't going to help them," Ellie argued shaking her head.

It was the middle of the night, the rain had stopped, and she and Jeff had drunk two pots of coffee between them. "They're packed every day, so extra bodies aren't going to help."

"Maybe they could look at getting their overheads down to help recoup the rent increase?" Jeff suggested.

Ellie shook her head, overwhelmed with the task before them. "I don't think so. Food costs what it does, and staff need to be paid. We ask a restaurant of Thasos' calibre to get their chicken from a can and they'll die long before their landlord moves in."

"Couldn't they increase what they charge per cover then? Current menu prices are more than reasonable."

"Yes, but Jeff, these are all things Chris himself would surely know to do— not to mention his parents. He likely hasn't increased prices because he already knows what his patrons can and will pay. Every restaurant has a sweet spot and Thasos likely found theirs a long time ago."

"But you said yourself he's given up and is facing the inevitable. We've got to do something. Come on, Ellie. Both our love lives our on the line here. Think, dammit."

"There's nothing we can do," she said, exhausted. "From a marketing perspective, we can only look at generating excitement for a place, but Thasos already has that and more. They're booked out every single night. If we want to help them, we need to go bigger. We need to..." She stopped.

Finally, something was coalescing in the back of her brain.

"Ellie?"

Lightning flashed outside, and the wind picked up. Rain was coming again.

"Ellie, talk to me."

But this time thunder was coming with it.

She had often complained that brilliant ideas never came. Well, no, that wasn't right. What she'd thought was that people themselves generally don't come up with brilliant ideas all on their own. They're simply receivers of information. Or in the right place at the right time.

Truly big ideas— *Moby Dick*, the Eiffel Tower, real eureka ideas— came from somewhere else. Somewhere *out there*, far beyond the human condition.

This particular idea wasn't hers either. She wouldn't take ownership of it in a million years because sometimes you had to give credit where it was due.

Thank you, was all Ellie could think when Mind (with a capital M) gave her a plan of action.

"Why did Zack send us here in the first place?" she asked Jeff, her mind racing.

"He wants to rule the world of course," her colleague replied deadpan.

"Specifically, he wants to rule *Greece*, or at least be known better here," Ellie went on. "But more importantly Zack Rose wants people all over the world to know that his kinsmen not only know him but admire and respect him, too."

Jeff sighed. "And the way he plans to go about that is by opening up his own restaurant here in Crete, but he doesn't want Thasos as competition so people will just come to him and not them. I know why we're here, Ellie," he said, confused.

"But really think about it. Do you think Zack truly cares about a restaurant here? When I was researching for this job, I learned that most of his money comes from ad revenue for the TV shows. The restaurants and the books merely maintain and rejuvenate excitement for his TV show."

Jeff nodded. "True. Without ad revenue funding his celebrity, he's just another cook."

"So what we have to do is take this to the TV show," she went on.

"And how in the hell are we going to do that?"

"Through Zack's ego, of course," Ellie said smiling. "You of all people should know that."

CHAPTER TWENTY-TWO

*E*llie wasn't allowed into the restaurant the following day but insisted enough that Chris finally came out to talk to her.

"Just listen," she said when he appeared in front of her, stony-faced. "I have an idea. But first, yes, I'll admit was asked to come here to spy on your restaurant and figure out what made you so successful. Zack Rose has a bit of a Borg personality and just wants to assimilate, assimilate, assimilate. Once he's assimilated, he destroys." She had hoped this might make him smile but she was wrong.

Still, he refused to meet her gaze.

"Chris, of *course,* the time you and I spent together was real," she said gently. "I could never fake how I feel for you. The butterflies you give me, the way you make me blush and speed up my heart." When he still didn't react to her essentially baring her soul, Ellie swallowed hard. "Anyway, things have changed. I've met you and your family and I won't let Zack destroy Thasos. But I need your help."

Now he looked interested. "How so?"

"What I need you to do is this: go on to Thasos social media today and announce a menu change. Make it a copy of the menu you designed for your other 'secret' restaurant."

Chris looked at her suspiciously. "But the people love the food my parents crafted here for the last thirty years. They don't want a change," he argued.

"This isn't about them. It's about *Zack*. But if you don't go along with what I'm planning, they'll get a change when you're out of business in a few weeks."

At this, Chris seemed to acquiesce a little. He sighed. "Continue."

"OK. I'm sorry but next, you will have to lie a little. Take full ownership of the new menu, but add that it is heavily influenced by the work and craft of your Greek kinsman, Zack Rose. Post this on your social media, and tag Zack - I'll help you with the details. Ask him to check out the new menu for himself, and give you feedback and advice. Talk about how much you've always admired him."

Chris looked horrified. "Why on earth would I do that? I know nothing about Zack Rose except he's an idiot celebrity who's trying to ruin my family's legacy. I certainly don't admire him."

"Like I said, you'll have to lie. The thing is Chris, all of this - Zack moving into Crete and destroying Thasos - it's all about his ego. He wants - *needs* - to be respected here, by his fellow countrymen. It's the only reason he's set his sights on your restaurant."

"Then he truly is an idiot. No true Greek would do such a thing to another."

"Well, you and I know that, but Zack doesn't. Again, this is all about him and his obsession with what people think about him. So I want you to mention him on Thasos' social media because he has a hugely active online presence - millions of followers."

"But why do you think this would do anything?" Chris asked. "Social media is—"

"About 80% of online communication these days. Trust me, Chris, if you want people to know something, you share it online. I'm telling you, I sat in Zack's office and listened to him gripe about Greeks not respecting him. All he wants is for his own people to flatter him. That's it. It's not about money; your restaurant is simply a means to an end for him. He's got fame, but what he truly wants is for his kinsmen to acknowledge him and call him brother."

"I'm going to need to check with my parents—"

"No, Chris. You're the boss. You make the call. This is how we keep Thasos from falling into the sea. This is how we keep it above water. Zack already has you in checkmate. The clock is counting down to your demise as we speak. We need to convince him that he's stronger with you than without you, and we need to do it soon."

CHAPTER TWENTY-THREE

The following day - using an ego-stroking spiel specifically crafted by Ellie - Thasos, one of the best-known traditional restaurants in Greece, paid tribute to Zack Rose, Crete's long lost son, asking him to visit them in person sometime, oversee the menu and ensure they got things right.

It was a masterstroke.

Ellie watched the interaction get retweeted and reposted around the foodie world in seconds, mostly due to Jeff's nimble administration of Zack's social media accounts.

While the hashtag of #ComeHomeZack, might have been a bit over the top - even for Jeff - she guessed that her boss would have no choice but to take notice.

Jeff and Ellie sat beside each other on her bed at the hotel that afternoon, watching Thasos' post go viral, waiting for their boss to react.

"GET BACK HERE - NOW," Zack demanded over the phone, barely an hour later.

"What's this about?" Ellie asked, feigning ignorance.

"You know well what this is about. I'm not an idiot, and neither are you. Get your ass back here pronto, and bring Jeff with you."

"Do you think he's going to fire us?" Ellie asked, hanging up.

Jeff looked up from his laptop. "Probably."

THE FOLLOWING DAY, Ellie texted Chris at the airport telling him that she had to leave and that she hoped to see him again one day.

Jeff had decided not to join her and had instead gone off in search of Patrick.

"I know you feel betrayed," she told Chris in the message.*"I understand that. And I know it's a cliche thing to say, but I tried so many times to tell you. I really did. It was*

selfish but I just didn't want to ruin what I hoped we might be developing.

If I could turn back time, and find a time portal like in that Stephen King book, I would. I wouldn't hesitate for a moment. This is my number. If you ever want to talk, please call me - regardless of what time it is. But for what it's worth, I think our plan worked a treat."

She left it at that. It was hard, but she knew he had every right to be angry with her.

Ellie had ruined everything.

Including no doubt, her brand new job.

CHAPTER TWENTY-FOUR

*T*he following morning, she was back in San Francisco and in front of Zack's desk.

"What the hell happened, Ellie? Spare me the bullshit. I know you're behind this ruse."

She faced him down, no longer caring about her job. She guessed she was going to get fired anyway.

"I realised Thasos wasn't what you wanted. The fate of the restaurant was the least of your concerns. So I had a brainwave."

"Which was?"

"What better way to show the world that your people love your work than to have a beloved native Greek restaurant pay homage to you."

"Hence the idiotic *Come Home Zack* hashtag?"

"Well that was Jeff's idea but…"

"So you seriously expect me to go all the way to Crete, sample their new Zack Rose-inspired menu, and give them the thumbs up?"

"Preferably with the TV show."

"But how does that help *me*?" he demanded. "I only see how it would help them."

"To everyone around the world, it will seem like you are a king visiting his subjects, doing a good turn for your fellow countrymen by putting Thasos even more on the map. Give them a good plug and your homeland will love you even more."

Zack pursed his lips. "If you're trying to save the place, know that the landlord will likely still want to raise their rent even if I back out. If it's not me, it's someone else. There are a lot of other businesses that would jump on that location."

"Then why don't we—"

"You're in love with him, aren't you?" Zack asked. "The manager. This is all a ploy to save *him*, isn't it?"

Ellie finally teared up. There was no point in lying. "Not all of it. But yes, I'll admit that I liked Chris - a lot. He and especially his parents ... they don't deserve what you'd planned. This way, you get what you want and they can stay in business. They're no threat to you, Zack, honestly."

The chef ran his hands through his spiky blond hair. He appeared slightly mollified.

"OK," he conceded sighing. "If this works out the way you think it's going to ... maybe I'll think about it. In the meantime, go home. I honestly don't know whether to fire you or give you a raise. I'll decide in a few days. Oh, and not that he cares, but tell Jeff he's fired. I can't believe he ran off with a Greek piano player. Talk about cliche ..."

Ellie texted Chris as soon as she was home and told him what Zack had said.

But once again, her message remained unanswered.

CHAPTER TWENTY-FIVE

*S*oon after, Zack got the go-ahead from his producers and sponsors to film a visit to Thasos in person for the TV show.

In the meantime, Ellie checked the restaurant's social media religiously to make sure the place was still open.

Business seemed to be carrying on as usual so if their landlord had indeed raised the rent, Chris and his parents must have all tightened their belts and were braving the storm.

When the visit to Crete eventually aired, it became the Zack Rose show's highest-rated episode ever. And as Ellie anticipated, the chef's fellow countrymen had little choice but to embrace him with open arms.

She watched the segment at Thasos over and over - especially the parts in which Chris appeared.

Incredibly, Zack didn't fire her. When he'd informed Ellie he'd decided to keep her on, he said it was only because a little voice within him had told him not to.

"I rarely get intuitions, Ellie. My brain and every fibre of my being told me to fire you, but it wasn't my brain that got me to where I am today. It was my intuition. So, by the skin of your teeth, you're safe. Now get the hell out of here."

Ellie tried to move on, and in one idiotic moment of self-pity she printed out that stupid picture of her asleep and wrapped around Chris on the aeroplane, and put it on her desk.

If nothing else, having it there was a constant reminder that she needed more out of life, and that there was someone out there for her.

If not Chris, then perhaps someone like him.

THEN ONE DAY, a Google Alert for Thasos announced that they had revealed to customers that the restaurant was going out of business.

The headline simply read, "Beloved Cretan restaurant Thasos closes its doors after 30 years in business."

Zack was having his morning coffee when Ellie barged into his office.

He put up his hand and said, "It's for the best. Their lawyers couldn't find a way to get the landlord to back off, and the owners - the parents - were ready to let it go."

"What about Chris?" she asked, lips quivering.

"I talked to him briefly. He's got plans of his own. You were right; he's a great restauranteur. Anyone would be lucky to get him."

That day, Ellie went home early. She texted Chris for the first time since the aftermath of her departure, telling him how sorry she was about the closure, and offering to do anything she could.

She'd also made a decision. It was impetuous and likely foolhardy but she was going to follow her heart.

"I know you don't want to see me, but I'm coming back to the island to talk to you. I need to see you - I'll do anything."

This time he texted back. "The best thing you can do for me is stay where you are."

Ellie's heart sank. It was the coldness of his response that did her in, morphing her sadness into a wave of heartbreak and disappointment that he truly didn't care about her.

Yes, he had every reason to be annoyed, but hadn't she done her best to make things right?

Clearly for Chris, Ellie's best wasn't good enough.

CHAPTER TWENTY-SIX

*T*he next morning, she decided to go into the office early.

Her brief interaction with Chris had left her battered and sore, but Ellie knew she needed to move on with her life as soon as she could.

She parked in the garage and walked around to the street entrance so as not to disturb Zack while he was recording.

Today though, the door to that entrance was locked. Ellie peered inside, hoping to see someone who could let her in, but she was obviously the first to arrive.

Reluctantly, she walked back to the attached parking garage, and went through that door, recalling her first day.

The same rat-like bespectacled sentry stopped her in the hallway and made circle motions in the air to tell her they were recording.

I know, I know.... Ellie slipped off her shoes.

The small man smiled and turned to escort her to the offices. As she followed him, she heard Zack in-studio talking to another person.

A man with a thick accent and warm lyrical tones that Ellie would recognise anywhere. She stopped short and looked into the studio.

Her boss was standing to the side and watching none other than *Chris* making bread.

"What's the grain called again?" Zack was asking.

"Kamut. K, A, M, U, T. If you are gluten intolerant, don't bother working with it, but if you are merely sensitive to gluten, give it a try. Here I see so many gluten-free products in your grocery stores. In Greece, we don't cook with American grains. We use the old grains, and very few of us have trouble with gluten. Go into one of our grocery stores and you won't find entire shelves and aisles devoted to gluten-free products. I give you no guarantee it will work, but try it. Take little bites. Listen to your body. You'll know if you can eat it pretty quickly."

Zack looked at the camera and raised his eyebrows. "Give it a shot, folks. Only don't sue the network if anything happens." At this, both men laughed. "If you're just tuning in, my friend Chris here is making us some Greek bread with a twist— he's using Kamut flour instead of traditional ..."

Not caring they were recording, Ellie burst through the studio doors.

"You're here!" she gasped to Chris. "What are you doing *here?*"

Out of the corner of her eye, she saw Zack motion to the production team.

Chris looked back at her, grinning wickedly as if he'd fully expected Ellie to walk onto the set in the middle of the show. "My parents and I eventually realised it was the best thing to happen for all of us. They've finally retired and I'm charging ahead with my restaurant — it's no longer just an experiment. We've added a modern building around my grandfather's old hut, and have most of the cooks from Thasos. We're not even open yet, and we're booked solid for our first three months."

"Who's *we?*" Ellie asked, overwhelmed but happy for him. "And what are you doing here?"

"Zack. He's my patron, the one funding all of it." She looked around for her boss but didn't see him. "So I came here to America to help return the favour - and something else of course."

She looked at him mystified. Chris and Zack teaming up? Why hadn't her boss said anything?

"Ellie," Chris continued, moving towards her, "I have everything I need to get started with my new business except one thing - a marketing guru. Know anyone who might be any good?" he asked, eyes twinkling. "And most importantly, someone who'd be willing to make a go of it with me - on an island in the sun?"

Without saying anything, Ellie melted into his arms, gripping the front of his shirt, afraid to let go in case all of this was a dream.

"I thought ... I thought you hated me..." she whispered, drinking in his scent, unable to believe that he was really here, and not only that, but he wanted her to go back to Crete with him.

Ellie didn't even need to think about that - she'd do it in a heartbeat. He was the one for her; there was no question about that. What's more, her subconscious had known it even before she did - right from the very beginning on the flight.

"Kiss him!" Zack shouted from the shadows then. "So we can call this a wrap."

She did so, not needing to be asked twice.

But for Ellie and Chris, it wasn't a wrap.

It was just the beginning.

ALSO AVAILABLE

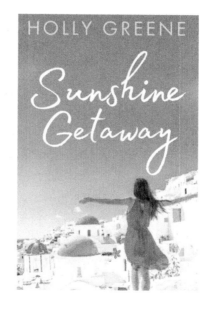

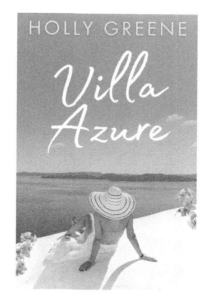

ALSO AVAILABLE

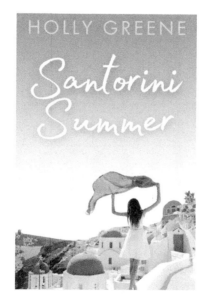

MORE BY HOLLY GREENE

Escape to Italy Series

Escape to the Islands Series

Printed in Great Britain
by Amazon

43086150R00081